Jabba the Hutt's Father Has Returned!

Zorba the Hutt clutched his chest. "Dead?" Was his heart going to explode? "My son . . . *dead?*"

Zorba let out a wheezing sigh of grief that vibrated the whole room. "How did Jabba die?" he demanded.

"He was murdered by Princess Leia," a Jenet said, scratching the white fuzz that covered his body.

"She killed him in cold blood!" Tibor shouted, pounding his body armor with a green fist.

"Princess Leia was Jabba's slave," the Twi'lek alien explained. "She had a chain attached to her. And she took the chain like this . . ." The Twi'lek twisted his own tentacle about his neck, to demonstrate. "And she squeezed the breath out of Jabba. It happened in his sail barge at the Great Pit of Carkoon."

Zorba's yellow eyes bulged from their sockets. "In the name of the ancient conqueror, Kossak the Hutt, I swear that this Princess Leia shall die!"

ZORBA ᵀᴴᴱ HUTT'S REVENGE

The Adventure Continues...

titles in Large-Print Editions:

Book 3

ZORBA THE HUTT'S REVENGE

PAUL DAVIDS
AND HOLLACE DAVIDS

Illustrated by Karl Kesel

Gareth Stevens Publishing
MILWAUKEE

For a free color catalog describing Gareth Stevens' list of high-quality books
and multimedia programs, call 1-800-542-2595 (USA) or 1-800-461-9120
(Canada). Gareth Stevens Publishing's Fax: (414) 225-0377.
See our catalog, too, on the World Wide Web: http://gsinc.com

Library of Congress Cataloging-in-Publication Data

Davids, Paul.
    Zorba the Hutt's revenge / Paul Davids and Hollace Davids.
       p. cm. — (Star wars)
    Summary: While the villainous Trioculus plots to steal away Princess Leia from
Han Solo and make her his dark queen, Jabba the Hutt's father Zorba prepares to
avenge the death of his son at Leia's hand. ·
    ISBN 0-8368-1991-8 (lib. bdg.)
    [1. Science fiction.] I. Davids, Hollace. II. Title. III. Series: Davids, Paul.
Star wars.
PZ7.D282355Zo 1997
[Fic]—dc21   97-21969

This edition first published in 1997 by
Gareth Stevens Publishing
1555 North RiverCenter Drive, Suite 201
Milwaukee, Wisconsin 53212 USA

Original © 1992 by LucasFilm, Ltd. Published by arrangement with Bantam
Doubleday Dell Books for Young Readers, a division of Bantam Doubleday
Dell Publishing Group, Inc., New York, New York. All rights reserved.

Cover art by Drew Struzan
Interior illustrations by Karl Kesel

Printed in the United States of America

1 2 3 4 5 6 7 8 9 01 00 99 98 97

To Matthew, Julie, and Colin Dwyer,
and to Michael, Max, and Sam Goodman,
May your dreams always fly
  with the *Millennium Falcon* . . .

Acknowledgments

With thanks to George Lucas, the creator of Star Wars, to Lucy Wilson for her devoted guidance, to Charles Kochman for his unfailing insight, and to West End Games for their wonderful Star Wars sourcebooks—also to Betsy Gould, Judy Gitenstein, Peter Miller, and Richard A. Rosen for their advice and help.

The Rebel Alliance

Luke Skywalker

Princess Leia

Han Solo

Chewbacca

Ken

Chip

Lando Calrissian

Kate (KT-18)

The Empire

Trioculus

Grand Moff Hissa

Zorba the Hutt

Tibor

CB-99

Twi'lek alien

Supreme Prophet Kadann

Triclops

A long time ago,
in a galaxy
far, far away...

The Adventure Continues . . .

It was an era of darkness, a time when the evil Empire ruled the galaxy. Fear and terror spread across every planet and moon as the Empire tried to crush all who resisted—but still the Rebel Alliance survived.

The Rebel Alliance was formed by heroic men, women, and aliens, united against the Empire in their valiant fight to restore freedom and justice to the galaxy.

Luke Skywalker joined the Alliance after his uncle purchased a pair of droids known as See-Threepio (C-3PO) and Artoo-Detoo (R2-D2). The droids were on a mission to save the beautiful Princess Leia. Leia, an Alliance leader, was a captive of the Empire.

In his quest to save Princess Leia, Luke was assisted by Han Solo, the dashing pilot of the spaceship *Millennium Falcon,* and Han's copilot, Chewbacca, a hairy alien known as a Wookiee.

Han and Luke eventually succeeded in rescuing the Rebel Princess, but their struggle against the Empire did not end there. Luke and his ragtag group of Rebel freedom fighters battled armor-clad storm-troopers and mile-long star destroyers. Finally they destroyed two of the Empire's mightiest weapons: the

Imperial Death Stars, which were as big as moons, and powerful enough to explode entire planets.

In the course of his adventures Luke sought out the wise old hermit, Obi-Wan Kenobi, who became one of Luke's teachers in the ways of the Jedi Knights.

The Jedi Knights, an ancient society of brave and noble warriors, were the protectors of the Old Republic in the days before the Empire was formed. The Jedi believed that victory comes not just from physical strength but from a mysterious power called the Force.

The Force lies hidden deep within all things. It has two sides: one side that can be used for good, the other the Dark Side, a power of absolute evil.

Among those who followed the Dark Side were the two evil Imperial leaders—Darth Vader and Emperor Palpatine. After their deaths, a three-eyed mutant and tyrant rose to lead the Empire—Trioculus. However, he was an impostor who falsely claimed to be Emperor Palpatine's son. He was secretly in love with Princess Leia and hoped that one day he would persuade her to betray the Rebel Alliance and join the Empire as his queen.

Trioculus was warned by Kadann, the Supreme Prophet of the Dark Side, that his reign as Emperor would come to a sudden and tragic end if he failed to find and destroy a certain Jedi Prince. The prince, Ken, was only twelve years old. He was raised by droids in an underground city known as the Lost City of the Jedi. It was there, in the Jedi Library, that Ken had learned certain Imperial secrets that, if revealed, could threaten Trioculus's rule.

Trioculus was unable to find either Ken or the Lost City. However, Luke Skywalker was able to succeed where Trioculus had failed. Having located the Jedi Prince, Luke invited Ken to leave the underground city and join the Rebel Alliance.

Many creatures in the galaxy followed the treacherous path of the Dark Side—among them, a greedy alien gangster known as Jabba the Hutt. Jabba lived in a palace on the desert planet, Tatooine.

Han Solo should have known better than to do business with Jabba. Like all of the sluglike, ruthless Hutts, Jabba lived by the law of revenge. So when Han refused to pay his debts, Jabba offered to pay a rich reward to any bounty hunter who would bring him Han Solo—alive or dead!

Of the two choices, it was hard to say at the time which would have been more merciful for Han.

As it turned out, Han was delivered to Jabba alive—frozen alive—trapped inside a solid block of carbonite. In a state of suspended animation, Han was unable to move his body, and his mind was trapped in a terrifying, murky fog.

Jabba the Hutt decided to display the carbonite block that encased Han Solo. He hung it up in his palace like a trophy, for all his visitors to see.

With help from Luke Skywalker, See-Threepio, Artoo-Detoo, Chewbacca, Lando Calrissian, and Princess Leia, Han Solo was eventually rescued and revived.

In the meantime, the bloated Hutt had taken Princess Leia as his prisoner, keeping her chained beside him. But Leia was able to escape, killing Jabba in self defense. She twisted her chain around his fat neck, and kept on twisting it until Jabba gasped his final wretched breath. The galaxy was rid of that vicious, blubbering beast at last.

Though word of Jabba's death spread from planet to planet throughout the galaxy, the news never reached the dungeons of the mud-ball planet known as Kip. It was there on Kip that Zorba the Hutt had been imprisoned long ago for illegally mining precious gemstones.

But within the first year after Jabba the Hutt's death, Kip was conquered by alien pirates, and Zorba was released from prison. The pygmy aliens of the mud-ball planet had never figured out how to fly Zorba's spaceship, the *Zorba Express*. So the spaceship was still waiting for him, docked at the same muddy cliff where it had been left when Zorba was captured. He dug up his hidden supply of gemstones, and then climbed aboard his spaceship, setting his course for Tatooine.

Zorba fully expected to find his son Jabba alive and well, happy to welcome his father back to his palace. But a shocking surprise awaited Zorba. The fury of a Hutt was about to be unleashed—a fury known as Zorba the Hutt's revenge!

CHAPTER 1
The Droidfest of Tatooine

Luke Skywalker's Y-wing starfighter zoomed through deep space, on its way to Cloud City for Han Solo's housewarming party.

Han's sky house was finally built. It was now floating in the air two miles away from Cloud City, on the planet Bespin.

"I've got it!" Luke Skywalker exclaimed, as he adjusted their flight path. "I know what we can get Han as a housewarming gift. We'll get him an ultra-high-density household communication screen!"

The twelve-year-old Jedi Prince strapped into the seat alongside Luke shook his head no. "Sorry, Commander Skywalker," said Ken, "but Han already has two of them."

"Oh. Well, scratch that idea then," Luke said, disappointedly. "In fact, scratch all ten of the ideas I've come up with so far."

Ken closed his eyes, forcing himself to concentrate. What about getting Han a holo-projector? Or a deluxe power booster for one of his two cloud racing cars? Or what about a supercharged multidirectional laser blaster?

Suddenly Ken bolted upright, pulling against his straps. "I know what we should get Han!" he declared. "A housekeeping droid!"

"A housekeeping droid!" the golden droid, See-Threepio echoed. "Now there's a *brilliant* idea!"

"Droids make very practical gifts," added Microchip, Ken's silver droid whom Ken had called Chip for as long as either of them could remember.

"*Tzzzooop bcheeeech!*" tooted Artoo-Detoo, the barrel-shaped utility droid, signaling his agreement.

The vote from the three droids aboard the spaceship was unanimous: All in favor, none opposed.

"Well, I don't know," Luke said, knitting his eyebrows. "Han has been a bachelor all his life. Do you think he'd want a droid around to live with him?"

"What does being a bachelor have to do with it?"

Ken asked. "A housekeeping droid isn't like having a wife. It's just a robot."

"*Just* a robot?" Chip piped up, offended. "After all we droids have done for you, Ken, you call us *just* robots?"

"The fact of the matter is," replied Threepio, "Han Solo knows *nothing* about keeping a huge house clean. He'll need help desperately. He can't expect Chewbacca to be cleaning up after him all the time! Why, Han and Chewie can't even keep the cockpit of the *Millennium Falcon* straightened out! If you ask me, a housekeeping droid is the perfect solution."

"Okay, you've convinced me," Luke replied. "But now comes the hard part—choosing the droid."

Luke activated the star map on their navigation screen. "Artoo, cool the hyperdrive thruster power," Luke said. "We're going to glide straight into Mos Eisley Spaceport on Tatooine."

"Why do you want to land on Tatooine?" Ken asked, confused. "Aren't there droid discount stores near Han over in Cloud City?"

"I guess you've never heard of the Droidfest of Tatooine," Luke said. "That's the place to go. It's loaded with JDTs."

"What does JDT mean?" the boy inquired.

"Jawa Droid Traders," Luke explained. "The droidfest is the jawas' annual sale. They have the biggest selection of droids in the galaxy. And the best prices."

"Come to think of it, I read something about the

droidfest once," Ken said, nodding. "There was a file on it in the master computer, back in the Jedi Library."

Ken had learned many things from the files of the Jedi Library, practical things, such as how to repair a droid that has a glitch in its speech mechanism. And unusual things, such as why mynock bats that live on asteroids sometimes fly upside down.

And he'd also discovered some carefully guarded secrets—secrets of the Imperial High Command, secrets that even Trioculus, the evil three-eyed tyrant who now ruled the galactic Empire, would never want anyone else to know.

Dee-Jay, the droid who was Ken's teacher in the Lost City, had warned Ken not to reveal those secrets to *anyone*—including Commander Luke Skywalker, who was Ken's guardian now that Ken had departed from the Lost City and joined the Rebel Alliance.

It wasn't long before they landed on Tatooine, the planet with the twin suns where Luke had grown up.

They docked at Mos Eisley Spaceport, at a Y-wing landing bay. Then Luke, Ken, and the droids made their way through the crowd, bumping into aliens of all shapes and sizes in the corridors of the busy terminal.

At the landspeeder rental booth, Luke got them a vehicle that was large enough for their entire group—and with an empty seat in the back for the housekeeping droid.

As Luke steered above the burning sands, they

rode along swiftly on a cushion of air. In the distance Ken could see what looked like tall metal buildings.

"Those are sandcrawlers," Luke explained. "They're jawa vehicles with tank treads. They're parked for the droidfest, very close to the palace where Jabba the Hutt used to live."

"Who lives in Jabba's palace now?" Ken inquired.

"It's vacant," Luke said, "except for the Ranats that scurry around chewing on the furniture and drapes. You see, when Jabba died, they never found his will. So the government of Tatooine took possession of his palace. For awhile they turned it into the Tatooine Retirement Home for Aged Aliens. But there wasn't enough money in the budget to keep it open."

"Didn't Jabba the Hutt also own the Holiday Towers Hotel and Casino in Cloud City?" Ken asked, remembering something he had read in the Jedi Library.

"For a kid your age, you sure know your history," Luke said. "Jabba *did* own that casino. But when Jabba died, Holiday Towers was taken over by the government of Cloud City. My old friend, Lando Calrissian, runs it now. He's the governor of Cloud City."

The sandy plain near the vacant palace of Jabba the Hutt seemed to have as many droids as there were stars in the galaxy.

The JDTs had set up colorful tents in front of their huge sandcrawlers, showing off their droids and displaying their merchandise. Luke, Ken, and the three droids went from one tent to the next. The tents rippled in the breeze, like hundreds of waving flags.

They examined HSDs, Housekeeping Specialist Droids, of every size and description. They looked at male droids, female droids, old units, even brand new ones with every possible modern capability.

But one droid seemed to stand out above all the others—a female droid named KT-18. She didn't seem to be made of metal; her body was the color of a pearl. She was clearly a top-of-the-line HSD.

"Actually, nobody calls me KT-18," the female droid said in a nice voice. "I go by the name Kate."

"Kate," said Luke. "I like that. We're thinking of purchasing you to serve a good friend of ours," Luke explained. "He's a professional pilot. Have you ever met any Corellian cargo pilots before?"

"Dozens of them," Kate replied. "My first master repaired Corellian spaceships, and I met *all* the pilots who came into his shop. Before they met me, most of them were rude bachelors with no manners. But I straightened them out."

"Really?" Luke said, surprised.

"One of them even got married because of me. The last I heard, he had six children!"

"Well, Kate," Luke said, "if I buy you as a gift for Han Solo, you'd better lay low when it comes to giving him advice about manners and marriage and stuff like that. If you overdo it, he'll probably shut down your power unit and advertise you for resale."

See-Threepio got permission from the regional

manager of the Jawa Droid Traders to open up Kate's back panel and check the quality of her circuitry.

"Excellent microcircuits," Threepio declared. "Superb mobility, too. It's rare to find a female droid who's been manufactured with such quality and—"

"Now, Threepio," Luke interrupted. "I've read the manufacturing statistics. There's absolutely no difference between the quality of materials used to make male and female droids. I'm sorry if that's a blow to your pride."

"That's quite all right, Master Luke," said Threepio. "We droids have no pride. Only a sense of honor and duty."

The jawas knew Kate was worth a lot, and they drove a hard bargain for her.

Just as Luke finished making the deal, a cloud of swirling sand appeared from behind the old, empty palace of Jabba the Hutt.

But it wasn't a desert storm. The sand was being kicked up by the hooves of dozens of lumbering four-legged Banthas. The Banthas were beasts of burden, huge elephantlike creatures with big tusks. And on their backs were tall Tusken Raiders hollering war slogans and charging to attack with waving spears!

The regional manager of the JDTs began babbling frantically in the jawan language. "It's a land dispute," Threepio translated. "The sand people say this is their holy burial ground. But the jawas say this land used to belong to Jabba the Hutt, and so it now belongs to the government. They claim it's perfectly legal for them to hold their droidfest here."

Legal or not, the Tusken Raiders seemed determined to put a stop to the droidfest. Their Banthas trampled the jawas' tents. They kicked and stomped, knocked over droids, and speared several jawas. And then they went after Luke and Ken.

"Watch out, Ken!" Chip shouted.

Ken dodged a jawa spear, and it just barely missed him.

"Now you can see why none of us wanted you to leave the Lost City!" Chip cried frantically.

"Ken, get all our droids into a sandcrawler!" Luke shouted.

Ken quickly led their four panic-stricken droids, including Kate, into the shelter of a big, treaded vehicle.

Meanwhile, Luke fought on, outnumbered and surrounded.

CHAPTER 2
The Return of Zorba

Zorba the Hutt imagined the life of luxury that awaited him in his son Jabba's mighty palace.

It would be a life of rich, greasy foods, cooked in vats of Bantha fat and served in Jabba's banquet hall. There would be slaves to bathe him every month, relaxing in the pure, cool water that Jabba stole from the moisture farmers of Tatooine.

Zorba's old spaceship, the *Zorba Express*, approached the security sector near Jabba's palace on Tatooine. He activated his communicator, about to make contact with the palace and identify himself.

"Attention, Jabba, come in. It's your papa, Zorba. Do you read me? Over!"

But there was no reply. In the old days, Zorba thought, whenever he had requested permission to land, there had *always* been an immediate reply from Jabba.

What could this silence mean?

Zorba landed not far from the main entrance. He turned off the power in his craft, but the bell-shaped Huttian spaceship kept rumbling and clattering. *CHIZOOOOOK! SQUEEEEGE!* The ancient spaceship wheezed like a sigh from the chest of a dying Hutt.

Zorba squirmed out of the spaceship hatch. Then he began his slow crawl to the huge, thick front door of the palace.

When Zorba announced himself at the palace door, a mechanical eyeball popped out through a small opening.

"Please state the nature of your business," the mechanical eyeball said in a very businesslike tone.

"My business, as you call it, is that I am Jabba the Hutt's father, and I've come to see my son!"

"I'm sorry, Jabba the Hutt no longer lives here."

Zorba snorted. Obviously this mechanical eyeball was broken and in need of repair. Everybody knew that Jabba would never move from his palace.

"What do you mean Jabba no longer lives here?!" Zorba stormed.

"The palace is under new management," the mechanical eyeball replied. Then it moved here and there, studying Zorba from several directions. "Are you a Hutt?" it asked. "Indeed, you seem to be a Hutt!"

"Well, of course I'm a Hutt!!" Zorba shouted, his eyes bulging in anger. "How could Jabba's father be anything but a Hutt?"

"That's what I thought you said," the eyeball replied. "I'm sorry. No Hutts are allowed here anymore! New policy. No exceptions. Good day, sir!"

At that, the eyeball retreated and a metal cover slid into position to hide it.

Zorba pounded on the door. No Hutts allowed? Zorba had never heard of such an outrage!

Zorba knew that Hutts were disliked. Imperial officers often snickered whenever they talked about the planet Varl, the pockmarked planet where most Hutts lived. They said no alien creature of good breeding had ever been born on Varl. Once Zorba even heard an Imperial grand moff say that he considered Hutts to be immoral, nasty, domineering, and power hungry.

Zorba shuddered when he heard insults like that, because he considered them lies. Hutts were a proud sluglike species—very generous to their fellow Hutts, even if they were stingy and cruel to everyone else. And above all, they expected everyone—even mechanical eyeballs—to treat them with respect.

Zorba had to get to the bottom of this at once. He boarded the *Zorba Express*, and flew directly to Mos Eisley Spaceport, figuring that would be the best place to get information on the whereabouts of his son, Jabba.

Arriving at Mos Eisley, Zorba wobbled up to the big round doorway of the crowded cantina. Thanks to Jabba the Hutt, the new door was now big enough for Hutts. Jabba had threatened to shoot down one arriving spaceship each week unless the cantina door was enlarged so that he could fit inside. His request had gotten quick attention from the spaceport authorities.

As Zorba entered he noticed an Imperial grand moff standing by the bar of the cantina, talking to a group of alien bounty hunters. The grand moff was bald, with sharp, pointy teeth. He was pointing to a poster that said: WANTED BY EMPEROR TRIOCULUS! A JEDI PRINCE NAMED KEN FROM THE LOST CITY OF THE JEDI! GENEROUS REWARD!

"Grand Moff Hissa," said a Twi'lek alien, who had a long tentacle growing out of his head. "Do you know what this Prince Ken looks like? Or how old he is? Where does he come from? Did he get his name from Kenobi? Perhaps he is a relative of Obi-Wan?"

"I'm sorry, I'm not authorized to release that information," Grand Moff Hissa replied, seeming to cover up for the fact that he didn't know. "However, I *am* authorized to reveal that the Empire believes that Ken may have departed from the fourth moon of

Yavin with Luke Skywalker. The two of them are almost certainly traveling together!"

"AHEMMMM!"

Zorba cleared his throat. All eyes turned to look at his huge, wrinkled body, with its braided white hair and white beard. They stared at his enormous reptilian eyes, and his lipless mouth that spread from one side of his face to the other.

"I am Zorba the Hutt, father of Jabba! I want someone to tell me where I can find my son!"

An awkward hush settled over the noisy cantina.

"I was told that Hutts are no longer permitted in Jabba's palace!" Zorba exclaimed. "Who owns the palace, if not Jabba?"

A green-skinned bounty hunter named Tibor, a Barabel alien who was wearing a coat of armor over his reptilian skin, took a big gulp of his drink. "If I were you, Zorba," he said, "I'd calm down. Have yourself a drink of zoochberry juice."

"I will *not* calm down!" Zorba screamed. "I want information about Jabba! And I'll pay five gemstones to anyone who talks!"

The offer suddenly turned everyone in the cantina into an authority on Jabba. Dozens of voices began blurting out all sorts of things at once.

But there was one voice that stood out above all the others. "You seem to be about the only creature this side of the Dune Sea who doesn't know that Jabba the Hutt is dead," Grand Moff Hissa said.

Zorba clutched his chest. "Dead?" Was his heart

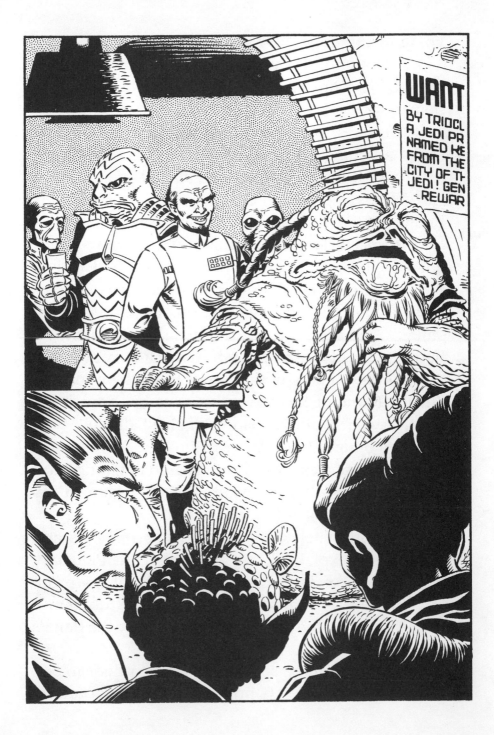

going to explode? "My son . . . *dead*?"

Zorba let out a wheezing sigh of grief that vibrated the whole room. "How did Jabba die?" he demanded.

"He was murdered by Princess Leia," a Jenet said, scratching the white fuzz that covered his body.

"Yes, it was Leia!" an Aqualish alien agreed.

"She killed him in cold blood!" Tibor shouted, pounding his body armor with a green fist.

"Princess Leia was Jabba's slave," the Twi'lek alien explained. "She had a chain attached to her. And she took the chain like this . . ." The Twi'lek twisted his own tentacle about his neck, to demonstrate. "And she squeezed the breath out of Jabba. It happened in his sail barge at the Great Pit of Carkoon."

Zorba's yellow eyes bulged from their sockets. "In the name of the ancient conqueror, Kossak the Hutt, I swear that this Princess Leia shall die!"

The bounty hunters murmured and exchanged approving glances. Then Zorba stared at Grand Moff Hissa. "Tell me, Grand Moff. Who is living in my son's palace?"

"Unfortunately, Jabba didn't leave a will," Grand Moff Hissa explained, "so naturally the Planetary Government of Tatooine took custody of his property—with the permission of the Empire, of course. At the moment, the palace is in ruins. Only the Ranats live there now."

"Ranats!" Zorba spit on the cantina floor in disgust. "I want ten bounty hunters!" Zorba announced.

"Ten strong men or aliens to come with me to Jabba's palace! I will pay seven gemstones each!"

There were more than ten volunteers. And each of them wanted to be paid before setting foot outside the cantina.

Zorba refused their request. "If any man or alien among you doesn't trust me to pay up once the job is done," Zorba threatened, "then I don't need you!"

The volunteers decided to take their chances. But all the way from the cantina to Jabba the Hutt's vacant palace, they argued among themselves about whether they had acted wisely. Most of them thought that they should have at least demanded a deposit of a few gemstones.

After a hot ride across the scalding desert in an old sail barge, they arrived at Jabba's palace.

Tibor aimed his portable anti-orbital ion cannon at the thick front door.

KABAAAMMMMM!!

The cannon blasted a hole in the door—a hole big enough for Zorba to squirm through.

Inside the palace, dozens of hairy Ranats scurried for safety at the sound of the explosion. They hid in the dark stairwells and palace closets, clutching their long rodent tails in terror.

The bounty hunters followed Zorba into the dry and dusty palace, which was in ruins. The Ranats had chewed the splendid Corellian carpets, clawed the expensive wall hangings from Bespin, and torn apart the custom furnishings from Alderaan so they could eat the stuffing.

In the palace banquet hall, it was too dark for the bounty hunters to see. And there was no longer any power in the ion surcharge generators.

But Zorba could see. His son had the walls of the palace built with ultraviolet luminous stones. Even though ultraviolet light is invisible to humans and most alien species, Hutts *are* able to see by ultraviolet light.

And so Zorba made his way to the far end of the banquet hall. There he opened a secret door, and then crawled into a hidden room.

With a gloating smile, Zorba reached out to touch a dusty old barrel-shaped droid that had been there since before Jabba was murdered.

He flipped a switch behind the droid's domed head. TZZZZZZT!

With the power turned on, the droid was reactivated.

"Zizeeeeep!" the droid tooted.

"Tell me, CB-99," said Zorba. "Do you still have all of your memory banks? Including file JTHW?"

"Zizoooop!" the droid beeped.

"Excellent. The fools! They shall learn that Jabba's will was here in his palace all along—right inside of you!"

Zorba gave a belly laugh—a laugh so deep and loud, one might have thought he was watching a prisoner being dropped into a vat of carbonite.

"A-HAW-HAW-HAWWWW! . . ."

CHAPTER 3
Han Solo's Housewarming Party

For hours Luke Skywalker and Ken had been listening to the *KA-CHANGGGGGING* sound of the treads of a hot, grinding sandcrawler.

The Tusken Raiders, whose weapons are quite primitive, were unable to force their way into the jawas' huge, cumbersome vehicle. When Luke had found himself outnumbered by the attacking sand people, he had taken the wise defensive action of leaping into the sandcrawler and slamming shut the thick, metal door. Ken and the droids, already safe inside, were relieved to see him.

Inside, the sandcrawler was hotter than a nanowave oven. Tatooine's twin suns nearly cooked Luke, Ken, and the droids.

"All I can say, Master Luke," Threepio commented in a whiny voice, "is that if you hadn't taken refuge in here with us, I'm afraid I'd be put up for sale to a new master come tomorrow morning."

This particular sandcrawler was one of a fleet of jawa sandcrawlers heading back to Mos Eisley Spaceport the long, slow way. But under the circumstances, it was the most practical way for Luke, Ken, Threepio,

Artoo, Chip, and Kate to escape and return to Luke's Y-wing starfighter, so they could still reach the planet Bespin in time for Han Solo's housewarming party.

By the time they reached Mos Eisley, it was nighttime. In fact, it was so late that the cantina was closed.

There wasn't even anyone on duty at the land-speeder rental desk. Luke left a note explaining that, due to a sudden attack by Tusken Raiders, he was forced to leave the landspeeder at the droidfest. He hoped the Tatooine Planetary Insurance Company would cover expenses for getting it back to Mos Eisley. If not, they could bill him on Yavin Four, care of SPIN—the Senate Planetary Intelligence Network.

But just as Luke, Ken, and the droids were approaching the docking bay where Luke's Y-wing was parked, two bounty hunters jumped out from the shadows with blasters drawn.

The bounty hunters, one of them a Twi'lek alien and the other an Aqualish, sprayed the area with laserfire. Instantly Luke drew his lightsaber and extended its blazing blade.

"Well, well, Luke Skywalker," said the Twi'lek, "just as expected." He wagged his tentacle with anticipation. "Trioculus has offered a reward for Ken, the Jedi Prince. He said he'd be with you!"

Luke leapt and did a somersault in midair, landing right between the two bounty hunters.

They never knew what hit them.

Luke swirled in a circle so fast that he was only

a blur in the corner of their eyes. His lightsaber struck them both in one swing.

CRASSSSSHH! The bounty hunters hit the ground at the same moment.

"Come on, let's go!" Luke said to Ken and the droids. "Before any of their friends get the same idea!"

Luke opened the hatch, and they all popped into the Y-wing, with Artoo-Detoo next to him in the copilot position. "Set course for Bespin, Artoo," Luke shouted.

"Bzoook!" Artoo beeped.

A moment later Luke activated the main thrusters. Their spaceship quickly departed from Tatooine.

When Tatooine seemed to be just a small glowing ball in outer space, floating between two fiery suns, Luke put the spaceship into hyperdrive. Then they quickly accelerated past the speed of light.

Luke glanced over at Ken. "Do you have any idea why Trioculus is after you?" he asked.

Ken shook his head no.

"That three-eyed dictator practically burned down all the rain forests on Yavin Four trying to find you," Luke went on. "Somehow he found out that you're traveling with me. He's even got every bounty hunter in the galaxy on your tail." Luke glanced at Ken's downcast face. "You must have *some* idea why he believes you to be such a threat to him."

Ken shook his head no again.

"But you do know, Ken," said Chip. "It's quite irregular for you to hide the truth from an officer of the Rebel Alliance. Especially a commander, like Luke

Skywalker, who's accepted the job of protecting you. Very irregular indeed."

Ken swallowed hard. "I'm a threat to Trioculus because I know too much about him."

"Such as?" Luke asked.

"Things I learned in the files of the Jedi Library—back in the Lost City," Ken answered mysteriously. "My droid teacher, Dee-Jay, told me I was not to tell anyone, Commander Skywalker— not even you."

"Not even me?" Luke said in a hurt voice. "What is there that you can't share with me, your guardian and protector? I take my responsibility to you very seriously."

"I'm sorry, Commander Skywalker," Ken replied. "But if I told you certain things, it would make your life even more dangerous than it already is."

Luke nodded, then clamped a hand on Ken's shoulder. "I understand, Ken," he said, though he didn't really understand. But he hoped that, in time, Ken would open up more and decide not to keep any secrets from him.

The planet Bespin was located just off the Corellian Trade Route. After Luke downshifted from hyperdrive, he pointed out Bespin's two largest moons, H'gaard and Drudonna. They were known as The Twins.

Bespin was aglow in a rainbow of color. Luke explained that it was a type of planet known as a gas giant, with a liquid metal core. The metal was rethin, and the core was called the Rethin Sea. The Rethin Sea was warm—not boiling hot, like the deep interior of most planets.

Most of Bespin was gas, or atmosphere. And Cloud City had been built to float in the sky of Bespin. It was held afloat by powerful repulsorlift generators.

The city was built in levels. At the top were the hotels, spas, clubs, shops, museums, and casinos. That's where the tourists and wealthy visiting gamblers stayed.

The lowest levels were called Port Town—a dangerous place, home of Cloud City's underworld; those levels were filled with bars and industrial loading docks. There were also casinos for sleazy gamblers and outcasts down on their luck.

As soon as Luke's Y-wing landed in Cloud City, they were met by Governor Lando Calrissian.

"Well, look who just dropped in from hyperspace," said Lando, his hands on his hips as he beamed a broad smile. "The Jedi Knight from Tatooine. And you've got company with you, Luke. Who's the short guy?"

"I'm tall for my age," Ken piped up. "They call me Ken."

"And they call me Baron Administrator Calrissian, Governor of Cloud City. But if you're a friend of Luke's, you can skip the formalities and call me Lando."

"Pleased to meet you, Lando," Ken said, reaching out to shake his hand.

As they spoke, Ken was distracted by a silvery

gleam from a hazy, distant cloud. It looked like a building floating in the sky.

"That wouldn't be Han's sky house by any chance, would it?" Ken asked, pointing toward what he saw.

"It would indeed," Lando said, grinning. "That faint, black speck in that swirling cloud over there is where Han camps out these days—Han Solo's personal stomping grounds in the sky."

Ken squinted and tried to pick out more details, but he could scarcely see the house, the air was so brown with haze.

"We call it *braze*," Lando explained, as if reading Ken's thoughts. "Short for brown haze. It's air pollution. And it's becoming a serious problem here in Cloud City."

Luke, Ken, and the four droids followed Lando, walking along a ramp toward Cloud City's fleet of

cloud car convertibles.

"Highly irregular to have brown air on a planet such as this," Chip commented.

"I certainly agree," Threepio added. "It's fortunate we droids aren't organic creatures. At least we don't have to *breathe* this discolored, chemical-ridden atmosphere."

"What causes the braze, Lando?" Ken asked.

"If you're looking for somebody to blame it on, blame Trioculus—the power-mad tyrant who's now running the Empire. Trioculus has stepped up war production on a huge factory barge floating on the liquid core of this planet."

"You mean on the Rethin Sea?" Ken asked.

"Bright kid," Lando said, shooting a glance at Luke. Then Lando looked back at Ken. "The Rethin Sea is full of rare metals and Tibanna gas," Lando continued, "and Trioculus is mining them to make Imperial war machines in his factories down below. He gets his mass-produced ion cannons, and we get stuck with the smelly braze." Lando sighed. "I sent him two messages asking him politely to please shut down and go away. But Trioculus doesn't understand the word 'polite.' He told me if I ask him again, he'll invade Cloud City and take us over."

Lando opened the door of a green cloud car convertible. "Well, friends, I'm loaning you an official government car for you to fly over to Han's party. Climb aboard."

"Aren't you going to the party with us, Lando?"

Luke asked.

"Later. Tell Han I'll be by in a few hours." Lando pointed toward a tall building—the Holiday Towers Hotel and Casino. "I've got some police business to check on. A greasy little Rodian alien has a new system for cheating at the card game of sabacc, and he's trying to break the bank at Holiday Towers again."

At Han's private cloud the spectacular housewarming party was already in full swing. A true intergalactic affair, there was dancing, music, friendly conversation, and plenty of zoochberry juice.

The floating sky mansion was filled with humans, aliens, and droids, all bumping into one another's elbows, claws, fins, flippers, and metal arms.

In the center, the most comfortable chair ever designed—a sort of gigantic floating pillow—was reserved for the guest of honor, Princess Leia. Her eyes were closed for the moment, letting the gentle rocking motion relax her and help her for a few moments to forget her worries about SPIN's plans and secret projects.

Beneath Leia's floating chair, Han was playing the role of a busy host, making sure that everyone's zoochberry glasses were full, and catching up with his buddies from his home planet, most of whom were bachelor Corellian cargo pilots. One by one he introduced everyone to Princess Leia.

Meanwhile, Admiral Ackbar, the sad-eyed Calamarian fishman, stood in front of the band and talked on and on about the military strategy that helped win the Battle of Endor for the Rebel Alliance.

But nobody was paying much attention to Admiral Ackbar—especially when Han began to open his housewarming gifts.

Every few minutes Han had to jump up and run to the kitchen to check on the gourmet feast he was cooking on his nanowave stove.

Then Chewbacca put on a chef's apron and took over the cooking, so Han could dance with Princess Leia.

The band knew all of Han's favorite Corellian folk dances. Han even taught Leia how to do the Space Pirate Boogie.

When they were both out of breath and laughing from dancing so hard, Han asked the band to play "Sweet Lady from Alderaan." He thought it would make Leia happy, because Alderaan was her home planet. But instead it brought tears to her eyes as she remembered how the Empire had used the Death Star to blow the entire planet of Alderaan to pieces.

Then Leia started coughing. "Are you all right, Princess?" Han asked, worriedly.

"It's the braze," she said. "The air pollution on Bespin seems to be getting worse."

"Chewie," Han shouted, poking his head into the kitchen. "Turn up the power on the repulsorlifts. Take the house up another hundred feet or so. The air will be cleaner up there . . ."

"Grooowwwrrr!" Chewie agreed, reaching for the repulsorlift controls over by the wide window that looked out on the brown sky.

"Han, you can't spend the rest of your life here going up higher and higher in the sky, trying to get away from the braze," Leia said. "That's just running away from the problem."

"Well, that's the code we Corellians live by," Han said with a laugh. "If you can't do anything about the problem, run!"

"It's not funny, Han," she replied. "What will you do when you get up so high that the air is too thin to breathe?"

Han shrugged. "I guess I'll worry about that day when it comes. And until then—how about another dance, Princess?"

And that's when Luke Skywalker and Ken showed up with the droids—Threepio, Artoo, Chip, and Kate.

When the hugs and hellos were over, Luke introduced Han to his housewarming gift. Han was overwhelmed. He asked Kate to demonstrate some of her modern housecleaning techniques. "Of course, Master Han," said Kate. "Do you see that stain way up in that corner of the ceiling?"

Han squinted and noticed the mark.

Kate fired a vaporizing beam from her fingertip. The stain instantly disintegrated. "A small sample of my many skills," said Kate. "But I'm best at washing dishes, cleaning windows, and restoring stained carpets."

"Incredible," Han said, proudly putting his hands on his hips.

Kate seemed to think just as highly of Han.

"You're the most handsome Corellian cargo pilot I've ever met," Kate said.

"Now don't get jealous, Leia," Han said with a mischievous grin. "Looks like you'll have to get used to the fact that I'll be living with another woman from now on."

"As long as she's a droid with metallic micro-circuits, I think I can keep my jealousy under control," Leia replied, with an equally mischievous grin.

As everyone got swept up in the excitement of the party again, Admiral Ackbar tried to snare Ken. He thought Ken would be a good audience for his war stories of how the Rebel Alliance blew up the Empire's Death Stars. But Ken tricked Threepio and Artoo-Detoo into keeping Ackbar company, while he and Chip ducked away to tour the house with Princess Leia.

"We can't even see the skyline of Cloud City with all this braze in the air," Ken said in a disappointed tone.

Then Leia noticed a new pair of long-range macro-binoculars that someone had given Han as a gift. They enabled a person to see details several miles away. She handed them to Ken. "Try these," she said.

Ken raised the macrobinoculars to his eyes and looked out the window. Suddenly, in spite of the braze, the view was incredibly clear. Ken could now see all the details of the distant skyline. Then he spotted a bell-shaped space vehicle approaching Cloud City.

"Hmmmmm. That's really unusual, Princess Leia.

I think I see a Huttian spaceship," Ken said.

"How do you know it's a Huttian spaceship?" Chip asked, as Luke came over beside them.

"Because I've studied spaceship designs back home," Ken said, lowering the macrobinoculars so he could see Luke. "It's shaped like a bell with a big door. It's large enough for a big, fat Hutt to get in or out."

"That's very strange," said Leia. "The Hutts almost never come to Cloud City anymore."

"Why not?" Ken asked.

"They used to come here all the time," Luke explained. "That was when Jabba the Hutt was alive and owned the Holiday Towers Hotel and Casino. But ever since Jabba died and Cloud City took over Holiday Towers, all the free-spending Hutt gamblers stopped coming here. They felt they weren't very welcome anymore."

"Here, take a look," Ken offered.

"Thanks," Luke said, taking the macrobinoculars.

Luke flipped a small button on the side of the macrobinoculars. Now they were powerful enough for him to read even the name on the side of the spaceship: *Zorba Express.*

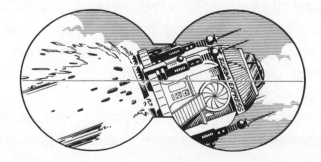

CHAPTER 4
A Friendly Game of Sabacc

The *Zorba Express* wobbled as it settled onto a landing bay in Cloud City.

CHIZOOOOOK! SQUEEEEEEEEEGE!

As the ancient, bell-shaped space voyager let out a long wheezing sound, the Cloud City Space Dock attendants exchanged an amazed look.

For an express spaceship, it certainly wouldn't be able to take many more express journeys. In fact, after a few more trips, it was doubtful it would even be able to break the sound barrier anymore.

From out of the hatch of the *Zorba Express* came a very odd trio. First came Zorba the Hutt, who at once began coughing, because of the braze.

Then came CB-99, the slightly bent, barrel-shaped droid following Zorba. He rolled along while Zorba squirmed his way across the wide platform.

Last came Tibor, the bounty hunter, his shiny armor strapped tightly around his horny green scales.

Their destination: The Holiday Towers Hotel and Casino.

Soon they entered the lobby, which was filled with noisy, glowing games of chance. This was where the rich gambled: slickly dressed aliens in colorful costumes, wealthy business beasts from the moons of Mima, and snobby humans who brought their droids along to pull the handles of the jingling Spin-and-Win machines.

Zorba attracted quite a few stares as he wobbled up to the main desk, licking the drool from his chin with his thick dark tongue. He began a conversation with a fancy clerk droid.

The clerk droid's body glittered with polished gems. Nothing but the best for the Holiday Towers Hotel and Casino. "May I help you, um, sir?" the clerk droid asked.

"I want the passkey to Jabba the Hutt's suite!" Zorba demanded. "It's the penthouse suite."

"I'm sorry, but the penthouse suite is no longer reserved for Jabba the Hutt," the clerk droid replied. "And I am not at liberty to give anyone the passkey."

Zorba scowled. "I won't put up with rude remarks from droids! You're speaking to Zorba the Hutt, Jabba's father! And Holiday Towers is now my property!"

"Perhaps you're not aware of the change of ownership of this establishment," the clerk droid responded. "The government of Cloud City took over this hotel and casino after Jabba the Hutt died." The droid's metal face gave a programmed metallic smile. "Governor Lando Calrissian runs Holiday Towers now. And he lives in the penthouse suite. I'm sorry, but I can't oblige you."

Zorba spit on the polished marble floor. "Notify that thief, Lando Calrissian, that Zorba the Hutt is waiting to talk to him! He'll find me at the sabacc tables!"

A short while later, Lando arrived at the game room in the lobby. As he approached the sabacc tables, he saw the huge Hutt with the braided white hair and white beard. And right alongside Zorba the Hutt were Tibor and the dusty, barrel-shaped droid, CB-99.

Zorba was playing sabacc, and he was losing. Lando watched Zorba open his pouch and take out some gemstones to buy more credits for gambling.

"Hello, I'm Governor Calrissian," Lando said,

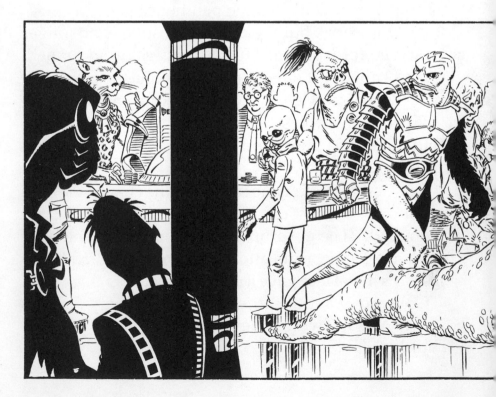

introducing himself.

Zorba's drooling tongue slid across his mouth as he hissed: "I'm Zorba, Jabba the Hutt's father. Get your things out of Jabba's penthouse suite now, because I'm moving in. And tell the clerk droid at the front desk to give me a passkey, or my friend Tibor here will send what's left of you to the nearest Cloud City mortuary."

Lando knew that there was no way to reason with a Hutt. The only way to get the better of a Hutt was to trick him, outsmart him, or wound his pride.

Lando had been around Cloud City casinos long enough to know how to recognize a miserable sabacc player when he saw one. And from the number of

gemstones he had seen Zorba lose, it was obvious that Zorba was an amateur, totally inexperienced at the game.

If Lando could talk Zorba into settling their dispute by playing a game of sabacc, then getting rid of this meddlesome Hutt would be a breeze.

"Tell you what, Zorba," Lando offered. "I'm a gambling man and a fair sport. I challenge you to a game of sabacc. If you lose, you agree to get out of the casino, leave Cloud City, and never come back."

"And if *you* lose the game," Zorba said to Lando, "*you* will leave Cloud City and never come back. And before you go, you'll appoint me as your replacement as governor! Do we have a bargain?"

Lando scratched his chin, thinking it over, recalling the time he'd gambled away the *Millennium Falcon* to Han Solo in a sabacc game. But Lando had learned a lot about sabacc since then. In fact, he was now the best player in Cloud City, second to none.

"We have a deal," Lando said with a grin.

Zorba spit into the palm of his right hand and held it out toward Lando. "Shake on it, then."

Lando's heart sank as he thought about having to touch Zorba's saliva-covered hand. He held up two fingers like a Junior Galaxy Scout. "What if I just say, 'Cross my heart and hope to die'?" Lando asked.

"Then you will die."

Reluctantly Lando spit into his own palm. And in the most disgusting moment of his life, Lando clasped Zorba's scale-covered hand and shook it.

Then Zorba opened up his pouch that had the gemstones and took out his own deck of sabacc cards.

"What's that deck for?" Lando asked.

"We play with *my* deck," Zorba replied.

"Now wait just a minute," Lando protested. "We're in the Holiday Towers Hotel and Casino. So we'll play with a deck that belongs to the house—"

Zorba wagged his fat tongue and chuckled. "I *own* the house," he said. "This is *my* casino, therefore we shall use *my* deck."

"You don't have any legal claim to this casino," Lando replied. "Jabba the Hutt died without a will. This hotel and casino automatically belongs to the government of Cloud City."

Zorba roared out a belly laugh.

"A-HAW-HAW-HAWWW! . . ."

Then, with his huge, glaring reptilian eyes, Zorba glanced at the barrel-shaped droid at his side. "CB-99, show Lando the hologram of your file called JTHW— *Jabba the Hutt's Will!*"

As instructed, the little droid projected a hologram into midair.

It showed the bloated, wrinkled face of Jabba the Hutt, reading his will. His instructions for what to do with his property upon his death were perfectly clear: *"Since I have no wife or children,"* the hologram of Jabba explained, *"if I should die before my dear father, then everything I own shall belong to Zorba the Hutt, including my palace on Tatooine, my hacienda in Mos Eisley City, the Holiday Towers Hotel and Casino in Cloud City, and—"*

The list of Jabba's possessions went on and on.

Then the hologram ended. And with it Lando's self-confident mood also ended.

Zorba laughed again, exposing the inside of his slimy mouth. "A-HAW-HAW-HAWWWW! . . ." he roared. "Just as I said, since *I* own the house, we shall play with *my* deck of sabacc cards!"

Lando's heart sank again. He inspected Zorba's deck—twice. And to his surprise, he couldn't find anything wrong with Zorba's sabacc cards.

Was it possible that it wasn't a rigged deck after all, Lando wondered?

Lando wasn't able to discover the answer. He did discover, however, that it was the worst day he had ever lived. He lost every single round of the game. His foolish bet had wrecked his life.

Lando didn't know—or even suspect—that Zorba had won because the deck had marks that could only be detected by a creature that could see ultraviolet light!

For the moment, all Lando knew was that within an hour of his losing, he was up in his penthouse suite for the last time, packing his things, ready to depart forever. And now Governor Zorba the Hutt was running the hotel and casino—and all of Cloud City!

CHAPTER 5
Trioculus's Factory Barge

Han Solo was disappointed that his party ended without Lando Calrissian ever showing up. But he was delighted with his housewarming gift, Kate, the housekeeping droid.

The guests departed, except for Han and Chewbacca's closest friends. And within two hours, the evidence of Kate's hard work could be seen in every room.

The floors were suction-cleaned, the dishes were sanitized, the trash was compacted and recycled, the leftover food was preserved in a cooling chamber, and thank-you messages were written for each and every single one of the presents Han had received.

"Roww-groooowwf!" Chewbacca howled, with a big smile.

"You're right, Chewie," said Han Solo, shaking his head in amazement. "No way that I could make it as a homeowner without the help of a housekeeping droid like Kate!" Han gave Luke a nudge. "Thanks a lot, old buddy. You sure had a good idea!"

"Don't thank *me* for the idea," Luke said. "Thank Ken. He thought of it."

"The idea just popped into my head," Ken explained, smiling. Both Luke and Han gave Ken an appreciative pat on the back.

"I hope you will all give credit where credit is due," piped up the golden droid, See-Threepio, in a jealous tone, turning to face Han. "*I* was the one who finally persuaded Luke of the merits of Ken's idea. I pointed out that you and Chewbacca seldom keep the cockpit of the *Millennium Falcon* neat and tidy. Without a housekeeping droid, in two weeks your house would end up looking like the trash compactor on board the Death Star. Do you remember when you were trapped in the trash compactor, and I said—"

"Yes, yes, I remember, I remember—" Han said quickly, shutting Threepio up. "My thanks to you, too, Threepio."

"*Bzeeepooosh!*" beeped Artoo-Detoo.

"And to you, too, Artoo," Han added. Then he put his arm around Princess Leia. "And Princess, thank you so much for coming. The party wouldn't have been the same without you."

"I wouldn't have missed it for anything," she replied. Leia smiled and gave Han a peck on the lips.

Han smiled back and gave her a long kiss in return.

BZZZZZZZZZZZZ!

Han's communication beeper was buzzing. Oh no, he thought. Who could be calling me now?

"Excuse me, folks," Han said. "I'll just be a minute."

Han went into his bedroom, where an ultrahigh-density household communication screen was located. He tuned in the large wall screen, and received the incoming message.

An image of Lando's face popped onto the screen, and he didn't look very happy.

"Sorry I missed your party, Han," Lando said. "But a whirlwind of trouble came along and set my head spinning."

"What's wrong, Lando?" asked Han.

"This is good-bye, old buddy. My political career in Cloud City has just come to an end!"

"What are you talking about? You can't just leave! You're Cloud City's governor!"

"I only wish that were true," said Lando. "I blew it, buddy. Remember how cocksure and self-confident I was the day I bet the *Millennium Falcon* and lost it to you in a sabacc game? Well, I had another attack of extreme self-confidence today—and I bet my position as governor in a game with Zorba the Hutt, Jabba the Hutt's old man."

Han's mouth fell open. "Jabba the Hutt's father? That old slug? Nobody's seen him for years!"

"Well, he's back. And the bad news is, he aced me. So Zorba is your new governor. Cloud City is sure to go to ruin." Lando glanced at his watch. "I'm on my way. My bags are packed, and my spaceship for the Zabian System is all set to leave."

"But what'll you do, Lando? You're out of a job!"

"Don't worry about me," Lando replied. "I've

still got a few tricks up my sleeve. I've been thinking about trying my hand at the theme park business."

A shocked expression swept over Lando's face. He could no longer put off telling Han the worst news of all. "Han, I overheard Zorba talking. He found out that Princess Leia killed Jabba. He's got the look of revenge in his big, ugly reptilian eyeballs. Whatever you do, don't let him find out that Leia is here on the planet, or she's a goner, for sure!"

CLICK!! The screen went black. It was the end of the message.

All the color was drained from Han's face. He called Luke and Leia into the bedroom and told them the news in private.

"We'd better get you off this planet, Leia—and fast!" Han said. "With Zorba out for revenge, he won't be satisfied until he succeeds. And if he manages to get his big ugly Hutt hands on you, it's your funeral!"

Suddenly, on the other side of the door, they heard Ken scream out, "Oh no! Kate!" Then Ken came bursting into the bedroom without even knocking. "Commander Skywalker!" Ken yelled frantically. "Kate fell!"

"What? Fell? How?" Luke asked.

"She was outside cleaning the observation balcony," Ken explained. "And she leaned over and fell into the clouds!"

"I'm going after her!" Luke shouted.

Luke hurried out the front door and walked along the yard platform. Struggling to keep his balance, he headed for the cloud car convertible he had borrowed from Lando, taking Han's macrobinoculars with him.

Luke leapt into the car. Then someone jumped into the seat alongside him. "Leia. But I thought you'd stay behind and—"

"Move it, Luke. Or she'll be halfway down to the Rethin Sea."

Luke powered up. *WHOOOOOOSH!*

The cloud car took off and plunged down into the clouds at a steep angle, straight into the thick braze.

Luke triggered the hyperaccelerator. Now they were zooming faster than a droid would fall.

Luke aimed the cloud car pointing straight down, and accelerated even more.

Soon, through the misty braze, they could see Kate falling down below.

Once Luke had been saved from a fall at the bottom of Cloud City. He had tumbled right into the hatch of the *Millennium Falcon* as it flew underneath to rescue him.

Now he used the same strategy to rescue Kate. He flew the cloud car convertible beneath her, adjusted his angle and speed, and ever so gently she plopped right into the back seat.

"How can I ever thank you?" Kate asked, calmly. "But what will Master Han Solo say? I fell down on the job."

"You sure did," Princess Leia said. She pointed straight down, as the cloud car convertible kept descending. "You fell practically all the way down to the Rethin Sea. Look down below—there's the liquid metal core of the planet."

"And look over there!" Luke said excitedly. "There's Trioculus's factory barge!"

The barge was vast—a huge metal platform floating above the Rethin Sea. And on the platform were several dozen enormous factories.

The barge was an Imperial base for making weapons and ammunition—antivehicle laser cannons, Comar tritracker artillery, anti-orbital ion cannons, field missile launchers, and turbolaser emplacements. All molded from rethin and other metals found in Bespin's liquid core.

Towering above the factory barge were smokestacks, thick and tall, spewing out foul clouds of brown gas.

"Now that we're here, let's take a closer look," Princess Leia suggested.

"How about some other time?" Luke said.

"We're this close, Luke. We might as well see if we can come up with any ideas on how to stop this braze."

Luke reluctantly agreed. It was a bold idea on Leia's part. Maybe too bold, Luke thought.

As they flew nearer, their cloud car was observed down below. Suddenly the laser defense system of the factory barge came to life.

Luke swerved to dodge the blasts, but he was much better at piloting spaceships and landspeeders than cloud cars. They were hit.

The underside of their vehicle was cracked down the middle. For the moment Luke still had control, but they were losing altitude fast.

Steering frantically, Luke made their car weave in and out among the smokestacks. The car took another hit from laserfire, and within seconds, it smashed into the barge.

SCREEEEEECH! came the sounds of metal scraping metal.

The cloud car convertible skidded along a road on the factory barge. At last it came to a crashing halt, right in front of a factory covered with brown soot.

"Don't look now," Luke said, "but we've got

company coming up the road."

It was a vehicle full of Imperial stormtroopers policing the area, looking for the cloud car they'd just shot down.

In a flash, Luke, Leia, and Kate were out of the car, hurrying along the road on foot.

And just as fast the stormtroopers reached the wrecked cloud car, swarming all around it. Then they divided up to hunt for the passengers who'd escaped.

At the same moment, Luke suddenly spied their best hope for safety—a narrow tunnel with a ladder that went straight down, a sort of passageway underneath the factory barge.

Kate popped down the tunnel first, to make sure the ladder was safe. Then Leia started to descend.

Luke sensed danger close behind him. Without hesitating, he drew his lightsaber, raising the bright green laser-sword threateningly. Three stormtroopers were fast approaching.

As Luke fought with two of the Imperials, the third strormtrooper reached into the tunnel and pulled Leia back up. From down below in the darkness, Kate could see Leia dangling and gritting her teeth, as the princess kicked and swung her arms.

Leia's feet reached the safety of the metal floor of the factory barge, but her enemy had her in his grip. No sooner had Luke toppled one of their foes with his lightsaber, than he felt another one of the stormtroopers shoving him, pushing him right down into the tunnel.

Luke plunged, reaching out with one hand to

grab the rungs of the ladder.

"Oh no, Commander Skywalker," Kate screamed, "you're going to—"

But before he toppled into Kate, Luke broke his fall, just in time to see the stormtrooper slam a metal cover over the top of the tunnel, leaving them in total darkness.

CHOOOIIIIIING!

A clamp twisted over the tunnel cover. Outside, on the surface of the factory barge, the stormtrooper who held Leia then turned a valve.

"Luke!" Leia screamed, her voice muffled by the metal.

TCCHHHHHHHHH . . . Poisonous gas flowed from the factory, through the valve, down a pipe, and directly into the tunnel.

In the darkness, Luke climbed the ladder and pounded on the cover that sealed him in. But it was closed tight. There was no way out.

"You're an organic creature, you have to breathe!" Kate exclaimed. "But if you breathe the poison, you'll die!"

Luke held his breath, closed his eyes, and concentrated. He focused his thoughts on the Force.

Luke knew how to move objects using the Force. He had learned how to do it in Yoda's swamp back on the planet Dagobah, while training to be a Jedi Knight. Perhaps now he could use the power of the Force to move the latch that held the tunnel cover in place.

As Luke desperately held his breath, nothing

happened, at first. But then the Force was with him. The clamp holding the cover shut began slowly to slide loose.

Clinging to the ladder, Luke pushed up on the cover. Then he leapt out and gasped for air. Kate climbed up the ladder to follow him out.

Together they looked around in all directions, trying to find the princess. But the stormtroopers had taken Princess Leia away!

CHAPTER 6
A Tale of Two Captives

While Han was waiting for Luke and Leia to return with Kate, he showed Ken his two streamlined cloud racing cars in his cloud car garage. One was blue, the other red.

"If I enter the Cloud Car Racing Finals," Han explained, "I'll probably drive my blue car—the Custom Model-Q Foley." Han opened the door on the driver's side of the blue car. "Want to see what it feels like to sit at the controls?"

"Thanks, thanks a lot!" Ken said. And as he settled into the comfortable, cushioned seat, he asked Han, "How old do you have to be to get a license to drive a cloud car?"

"Eighteen for humans," replied Han. "Twenty if you're an alien. Except for Biths. They let Biths drive at age ten because they're advanced bipedal craniopoids who reach maturity at a young age."

"In that case, I wish I were a Bith," Ken said. "Say, what does this do?" He touched a green button near the steering mechanism.

FWEEEEP!

"That's the—whoops, too late," Han said.

The garage door opened. Through the braze Ken could see the distant skyline of Cloud City. The city seemed to be calling out to him, urging him to seek adventure.

Han leaned into the car to check the clock on the dashboard. "I'm getting worried about Luke and Princess Leia," he said. "They've been gone a couple of hours already. It shouldn't have taken them *this* long to rescue Kate and come back."

"Maybe they decided to stop off in Cloud City for a bite to eat," Ken suggested, putting his hands on the sleek, shiny steering mechanism.

"I certainly doubt it," said Han. "There was a ton of food at my party, and plenty of leftovers."

"But Princess Leia hardly touched a bite of your Corellian cooking," Ken said.

"Why was that?" Han asked, somewhat hurt.

"She says Corellian food is too fattening," Ken explained.

"Oh, yeah?" Han said, glancing down to see if he was getting a pot belly. "You don't see any fat on *me*!"

Suddenly Chewbacca poked his head through the door to the garage. "Rowwwwrf! Groouuuuf!" he moaned.

"You're kidding!" Han said to his Wookiee friend, then glanced back at Ken. "Luke sent us a distress call. They're in some kind of trouble. My beeper was turned off, so we didn't get the message until Chewie here checked the machine just now."

Han put a hand on Ken's shoulder and said,

"Wait here, kid. I'll be back in a flash."

But Han didn't come back in a flash.

So Ken decided to pretend he was driving the cloud racing car he was sitting in. He gripped the controls. He leaned forward. And he put his hand on the acceleration lever, touching it ever so lightly.

But the light touch was all it took to power up the car and send it zooming out of the garage, into the open sky, and off toward Cloud City.

In the Jedi Library, Ken had spent many hours reading about how to fly cloud racing cars. Now he was able to make a couple of wide loops, spinning rolls, and upside-down maneuvers, all for real.

Before he knew it, he was almost all the way to Cloud City. And he almost collided in midair with a cloud bus.

OOOOO-EEEEE! . . . OOOOO-EEEEE! . . .

A Cloud Police siren blared loudly.

The police car aimed an invisible tractor beam at the cloud racing car Ken was driving.

Ken was towed to a landing bay at Cloud City. "You sure don't look eighteen, kid," one of the Cloud Police said. "Do you have the registration for this vehicle?"

"This was all just a mistake, officers," Ken said.

Ken explained that he had come to Bespin with Luke Skywalker. And that he had been driving Han Solo's cloud car totally by accident.

"Trioculus offered a big reward for a Jedi Prince named Ken who's been traveling with Luke Skywalker,"

one of the Cloud Police said to the other. "There're Wanted posters for this kid on at least a dozen planets."

And so they arrested Ken for reckless driving without a license. His destination: Cloud City Police Headquarters.

Back at Han's sky house, Han was frantic.

"Threepio, take my red cloud racing car—the Model-X1 Zhurst," Han ordered. "Bring Artoo and Chip with you, and go find Ken. He's probably taken off for Cloud City. Chewie and I will take a ride in the *Millennium Falcon* to find out what happened to Luke, Leia, and Kate!"

On the factory barge, Princess Leia was inside Trioculus's private chamber, high up in the tallest of his factories. The room had modern Imperial art and elegant furniture.

The three-eyed tyrant, Trioculus, gave a sly smile as he stared at his lovely captive.

"Please be seated, Princess Leia," he said, trying to make his gruff voice sound pleasant. "I hope you'll find these quarters comfortable."

Leia refused his invitation to sit. Instead she stared out the window, trying to avoid looking at him.

"What's happened to Luke?" she asked nervously.

"A most unfortunate situation," Trioculus replied soothingly. "We made every effort to save his life, but alas, it was to no avail."

"Do you expect me to believe that Luke is dead?" she said angrily, turning to look at Trioculus's three eyes.

"Sadly, your Luke Skywalker has departed from the world of the living," Trioculus explained. "But if it's any consolation, he died a quick and painless death."

"I don't believe a word you're saying," Leia snapped. "I would know it if Luke were dead. I would feel it."

"Perhaps not. Down here, by the Rethin Sea, feelings are dulled. All feelings—that is except my feelings for *you*, Princess Leia!"

"You don't *have* any feelings," she said. "You're a murderer! A liar! An inhuman monster!"

In a fit of fury, Leia slapped his face. Trioculus just stood there, watching her without stirring.

Leia cringed as she looked at the Imperial ruler. She had seen holograms of him in intelligence briefings, and when Trioculus sent a personal warning to the SPIN conference room in the Rebel Alliance Senate. The holograms had depicted Trioculus as devious but handsome. Handsome, except for the strange, mutant third eye in the middle of his forehead. But now his face was scarred.

She looked away, unable to bear the sight of him. However, Trioculus couldn't take his three eyes off her. He found Leia's strong but soft features to be beautiful.

Trioculus was convinced that in time he might be

able to bridge the gap between their opposite worlds. If she stayed with him long enough, eventually she might renounce the Rebel Alliance. And perhaps then she would even come to accept the necessity of evil. Especially if he were to marry her and make her the Queen of the Galactic Empire!

Trioculus took a few steps toward her. "Is it so wrong to be a murderer?" he asked. "Or a liar? Or an inhuman monster? I may be all of those things, but I still have a heart."

"Your heart is as dark as carbonite!" she hissed.

Trioculus glanced at his right hand, which now wore a replica of the glove of Darth Vader. He wondered if he should put that gloved hand on her shoulder, to show his affection for her.

"There can still be great beauty in a dark heart," Trioculus said, reaching out with the glove and gently touching her. The princess pulled away at once. "I'm certain there's darkness in you, Leia," he continued. "You're a murderer also. You killed Jabba the Hutt in cold blood, assassinated him with hatred in your heart. See yourself for what you really are!"

"I killed that thug Jabba in self-defense," she protested. "He was the most corrupt and vile gangster in the universe!"

"There's always an excuse the first time one murders," Trioculus said. "But the first murder is never the last. Why, I think you'd even like to murder me, right now. That's what you're thinking, isn't it, Leia?"

Trioculus put his hand on her shoulder once again. But she took it down right away. Then he squeezed her hand and didn't let go.

"I love you, Leia," he said in a fiery voice. "I want you to marry me and become the Queen of the Empire!"

Leia shuddered. "You're insane!" she replied.

"Accept me, Leia," he said. "I'm the only one who can give you the power and happiness you deserve!"

Leia pulled her hand away with disgust.

"You'll change your mind, Princess," Trioculus stated, refusing to lose hope that she would eventually accept his offer to be the Empire's dark queen. "There's still time for us," he said. "A great deal of time!"

CHAPTER 7
The Battle for Princess Leia

Zorba frowned as he stared out the window of his penthouse suite and slurped his sour brew. The braze outside was almost as thick as his drink, and the braze of Cloud City was the reason he had to drink the foul potion for his sinuses in the first place.

Something had to be done to persuade Trioculus to shut down his factory barge, or interplanetary tourists would find other planets that had casinos where they could spend their credits—planets that didn't have air pollution like the braze of Bespin.

Zorba had finished half his brew by the time Tibor came to see him. "I've just come from Port Town, Zorba," Tibor said excitedly. "I've learned some valuable information from an Imperial spy. Information that's worth at least five gemstones."

"Two gemstones," Zorba said. He reached into his pouch and tossed two valuable stones at Tibor's feet, as though they were no more important than glass marbles.

"Thank you, Zorba," Tibor said. "The murderess who killed Jabba the Hutt was taken captive by

Trioculus! At this very moment, Princess Leia is a prisoner on the Imperial factory barge!"

Zorba sputtered and spit out a mouthful of brew. This *was* exciting news.

"If only I had something Trioculus wanted badly," Zorba mused. "Something I could trade for the princess."

"I have an idea that's worth at least three more gemstones," Tibor offered.

"One more gemstone," Zorba corrected, as he reached into his pouch once again and tossed yet another stone onto the floor.

"Thank you, Zorba," Tibor said. "Here's my idea. I found out a little while ago that your Cloud Police arrested a boy who's been traveling with Luke Skywalker—a boy named Ken. Does that call something to mind, Zorba?"

"The Wanted poster in the Mos Eisley Cantina on Tatooine!" Zorba exclaimed. "Grand Moff Hissa said Trioculus would pay a generous reward for Ken!"

"Exactly, Zorba," said Tibor, "and what if the reward you demand is Princess Leia!"

Zorba laughed with delight. "A-HAW-HAW-HAW! . . ." But then Zorba stopped to think. "But what if this boy named Ken isn't the Jedi Prince Trioculus wants?"

To settle that matter, Ken would have to be questioned. And so Tibor took a message from Zorba to Cloud Police Headquarters, demanding that the boy be surrendered to Tibor so he could bring Ken to Zorba's penthouse suite.

Upon his arrival Ken was defiant. He threw back his shoulders, crossed his arms, and looked away from Zorba and Tibor.

But old Hutts like Zorba knew a lot about human child psychology. Zorba began the questioning by trying to make Ken feel at home.

"Such a shame a boy like you got into trouble," Zorba began. "Perhaps we can straighten it out. AHEMMM! My throat is so dry. I think I need a glass of imported Bantha milk. Bantha milk and cookies! How does that sound to you, Tibor?" he asked, winking at the bounty hunter.

"Sounds delicious," Tibor said, playing along.

"Does it sound delicious to you, too, Ken?" Zorba asked.

Ken considered his situation. Several hours had passed since Han's party. And he *was* getting hungry.

"Do you have any candy-flavored buns?" Ken asked. "I've always wanted to try them—or sticky sweetmallow?"

"Such a tasty idea! I was just going to suggest that!" Zorba lied.

He mumbled something to Tibor, whispering in the bounty hunter's ear. Then Tibor notified the Holiday Towers room service droids to bring up a tray of Bantha milk, sticky sweetmallow, and candy-flavored buns baked with avabush spice—a powerful truth serum!

When the snack arrived, Ken quickly gobbled down three candy-flavored buns!

Zorba talked on and on about how the braze of Bespin was having a bad effect on the tourist trade. And then, when Zorba felt he had waited long enough for the avabush spice to put Ken in a truthful and cooperative mood, he began by asking some serious questions.

"Tell me, my boy," Zorba said. "Are you a Jedi Prince?"

Ken brushed his moppy brown hair out of his eyes and said, "I don't know for sure, sir. I don't know who my parents were. The droids never told me."

"Which droids?" Zorba asked, rolling his big yellow eyes suspiciously.

"The droids who raised me."

"Raised you? Where?"

"In the Lost City of the . . . I mean, well, it was somewhere on Yavin Four. Or Yavin Three, I mean."

Zorba gave a devious smile. "Tell old Zorba the truth now. Hutts can get very nasty when boys lie."

"Yavin Four. I grew up in the Lost City of the Jedi," Ken continued, yawning as though he had suddenly become sleepy. "It's deep underground, in the middle of the rain forest. When I was little, I think my parents were killed in the Great War, but no one ever told me who they were. I think maybe my name, Ken, comes from *Ken*obi. I might be related to Obi-Wan Kenobi, but I don't know because the droids who raised me wouldn't tell me. All they told me was that a Jedi Knight in a brown robe took me to the Lost City for safety, so the Imperial stormtroopers wouldn't find me and . . ." Ken yawned again. "Do we have to talk about this anymore?" he asked. "I'm feeling so tired."

"You've told me enough," Zorba said. "There's no doubt about it. You're Ken, the Jedi Prince I've heard so much about." Zorba laughed with delight. "A-HAW-HAW-HAW! . . . Put him in one of the cells in the basement, where we keep the casino crooks we catch!" Zorba instructed.

"Of course, Zorba," Tibor replied.

"And then contact Trioculus on the factory barge. Tell him we have Ken, the Jedi Prince. Tell him if he still wants the boy, he should come to Cloud City so we can negotiate a deal!"

Zorba tossed one more gemstone at Tibor's feet.

"Thank you, Zorba!" Tibor said.

* * *

When Trioculus got the news, he locked Princess Leia alone in his factory barge chamber, leaving fine food and beverages for her. Then he departed for Cloud City at once, taking twenty stormtroopers with him as bodyguards.

Later that same afternoon, Trioculus and his bodyguards entered the Holiday Towers Hotel and Casino. The stormtroopers waited in the hall outside Zorba's penthouse suite, while Trioculus and Zorba bargained for their prisoners.

"I hear you are the new governor of Cloud City," Trioculus began. "Congratulations. I'm sure you will bring discipline and prosperity to the gambling industry here."

"And congratulations to you, Trioculus," said Zorba, "on becoming the new leader of the Galactic Empire."

The formalities out of the way, Trioculus then told Zorba he had come to make a deal for Ken. But first he wanted to meet Zorba's prisoner, to make certain he was actually the Jedi Prince.

Zorba instructed Tibor to take Trioculus to visit Ken in the cell in the Holiday Towers basement.

"A boy?" Trioculus said in surprise, as he first set his three eyes on the prisoner. "Why, you hardly look more than twelve or thirteen."

Ken pouted, refusing to reply.

Trioculus frowned. He had thought the Jedi Prince would be a man. How could this boy possibly be any great threat to his reign? But Kadann, the Supreme Prophet of the Dark Side, had warned Trioculus that he must quickly find the Jedi Prince named Ken and destroy him, or the Jedi Prince would destroy Trioculus! That was the prophecy. That was Trioculus's destiny!

"Don't be afraid of me," Trioculus said with a cunning smile. "I've come to Cloud City to help you. But first you must answer some questions."

Ken crossed his arms defiantly.

Trioculus heard static in his mind, static sent by Ken to attempt to cloud his thinking. And then Trioculus heard the words inside his mind: *I'm not the boy you're looking for!*

Trioculus frowned again. "Don't try those Jedi mind games on me, Ken. Stronger Jedi than you have tried and failed. It won't work," he said with a sneer. And then he changed his sneer into a smile.

"Did you learn that trick in the Jedi Library, in the Lost City of the Jedi?" Trioculus asked.

Ken grabbed the bars of the cell and narrowed his eyes in a glare of anger. "Do you think I'll talk to *you*, Trioculus? You're a liar, a killer, and a destructive monster!"

"You flatter me," said Trioculus with an evil grin. "Which do you think I excel at the most? Lying? I'm indeed an expert at deception. Killing? No, every slave lord has to hold an execution now and then, it's only natural. But now tell me, why do you consider me a monster?"

"You burned the rain forests on the fourth moon of Yavin!"

"I had to do what I did to try to find the Lost City. So I could find you."

"Perhaps the Jedi Prince would like another candy-flavored bun," Tibor offered sarcastically, handing the boy a bun through the bars of his cell.

Ken's stomach was still groaning with hunger. He munched on the bun as the three-eyed Imperial ruler asked Tibor to depart, so he could talk to the prisoner alone, in private.

Tibor left as requested.

To foil spies and secret listening devices, Trioculus activated a small sound-wave scrambler he carried in his pocket. It would assure that no one else would hear what they were saying.

Ken yawned once more, feeling tired again. "Why did you want to find me?" Ken asked.

"Why, to become your protector, of course," Trioculus replied. "So you could leave the droids who raised you and be free."

Ken's eyelids felt weighted down, dragging him once again into sleep. What had Trioculus just said, he wondered? Things were becoming foggy. Uhmm—something about wanting to become Ken's protector . . .

"You—you don't care about me," Ken declared, struggling to remain awake. "You're a liar. I know why you've been looking for me. You want to destroy me because I know too much!"

"What do you think you know that I would care about?" Trioculus asked in a cagey tone.

"I know that you got to be ruler of the Empire by pretending you're Emperor Palpatine's son. But you're not. You're an impostor! I even know what you did to the Emperor's real son, Triclops. And that he's still alive!"

All three of Trioculus's eyes widened in alarm. "Such an imagination for a boy your age. You have a head full of absurd fantasies."

"You know I'm telling the truth. And if you try to hurt me, I'll escape and tell *everything* I know about you!"

"Who would you tell?" Trioculus asked.

"Kadann, the Supreme Prophet of the Dark Side," Ken said.

"Nothing escapes Kadann's attention," Trioculus said. "I sincerely doubt you could tell him anything he hasn't already foreseen in his prophecies."

"Then I'll tell all your enemies in the Empire! If they ever find out the truth about you, they'll assassinate you!"

Trioculus understood at once that this Jedi Prince *would* have to be destroyed, at any cost. If some of his enemies, who didn't know any better, were to find out the truth, they would begin a search for the Emperor's *real* son, and try to put that insane madman in power.

Trioculus had to stop that from happening. Palpatine's real son, Triclops, was too dangerous and destructive for even the Empire to tolerate. Trioculus and the Central Committee of Grand Moffs knew all too well that Triclops was incurably insane and a terrible threat. They had managed to imprison and hide him in Imperial insane asylums. But they knew it would be unwise to destroy him, because Triclops often betrayed himself. In his mad dreams, he had come up with many ideas that had proved useful to the Empire. His ideas—and inventions—had been essential to them for building certain weapons and machines of destruction.

"You're a young boy with strong opinions and dangerous ideas," Trioculus said, his voice suddenly becoming very gruff. "We shall meet again, Jedi Prince Ken. Very soon!"

Trioculus went back to see Zorba the Hutt at once.

"I want that boy," Trioculus said. "What is your price?"

Zorba gave a slobbering smile and chuckled. "I want just two things."

Trioculus clenched his fists. "Name them."

"Number one," said Zorba. "I want you to close down your factory barge here. Your smokestacks cause braze."

"A little braze never harmed anyone," Trioculus insisted.

"Hah!" Zorba exclaimed. "Hutts can't stand braze, and neither can tourists." Zorba wagged his fat tongue at Trioculus scoldingly. "Business in the

casinos is down—*way* down—even though we're of-
fering bigger jackpots than ever! Braze is driving our
customers away—no one wants to come to Cloud
City and breathe your foul smoke!"

"And the second thing?" said Trioculus, giving no
hint of what his response would be to the first demand.

"Princess Leia. I know you have her. She murdered my son, Jabba, and she will pay with her life."

Trioculus knitted his eyebrows and frowned.
"No. You cannot have Princess Leia."

Zorba pounded his right fist into his left palm.
"Leia for Ken! One human traded for another! Fair is
fair!"

"No," said Trioculus.

Zorba's pale, wrinkled face became inflamed, turning a bright, fiery red. "Yes!" Zorba hissed.

"No!" stormed Trioculus.

"Yes, yes, yes!! I am a Hutt, and a Hutt does not allow the murder of his son to go unavenged!" Zorba snorted, snarled, sneered, and then asked, "What use is the Rebel Alliance princess to you?"

"She will be my wife," Trioculus declared in a gruff, angry voice. "She will be Queen of the Empire!"

Hearing those words, Zorba's old heart nearly burst.

"And when she's my queen," Trioculus contin-

ued, "there will be new taxes on every casino in Cloud City, starting with your Holiday Towers. Taxes for Queen Leia. So she can have anything her heart desires!"

Zorba's yellow, reptilian eyes turned up in shock. He wheezed like a creature about to die.

"I want Ken," Trioculus repeated. "And for Ken I will give you . . . a new spaceship. They say the old *Zorba Express* is ready to be made into scrap."

Zorba spit on the ground near Trioculus's feet.

"Curse you, you three-eyed mutant!" he growled. "You will *never* get Ken!"

Trioculus leaned forward, turning his hands into fists. "Give me Ken, now! Or I will destroy Cloud City!"

Zorba's eyes narrowed and glowed like yellow fire.

"We met as friends today. We congratulated each other. But from now until the end of time, you and I are sworn enemies! And once a Hutt makes an enemy, there is no retreat until death!"

"It is you who will die for this, Zorba," Trioculus threatened.

"May I never look upon your ugly, scarred face again," Zorba replied.

Trioculus pressed a button on the communication device on his belt. Seconds later, the door to the penthouse was smashed to pieces as Trioculus's stormtroopers burst into the room, their blasters drawn.

But Zorba was just as fast on the button. His

signal summoned an attack team of Cloud Police, hiding just beneath the floor. As a trapdoor popped open, the room was suddenly swarming with Zorba's henchmen.

The sound of Zorba's belly laugh echoed throughout the room. "A-HAW-HAW-HAW!! . . ."

CHAPTER 8
Revenge at Last!

Zorba's penthouse was filled with blazing laserfire.

In the fast fury of combat, Zorba was struck several times, leaving small, black scorch marks on his thick, wrinkled skin. But his skin was tough enough to protect him. And he didn't stop laughing for even a second.

Zorba's twinkling yellow eyes watched with glee as his Cloud City Police devastated the stormtroopers using their new model laser pistols.

A few stormtroopers escaped from the penthouse suite with their lives. They fled down the hall and were captured by a second group of Zorba's Cloud Police, who were just arriving on the top floor to serve as reinforcements.

The moment he realized that his defense forces were being defeated, Trioculus, half-crazed by the maddening sound of Zorba's laughter, tried to escape too. But he ran smack into three approaching Cloud Police. They overpowered the three-eyed Imperial tyrant, shackled him, and took him directly back to the penthouse suite, to face Zorba the Hutt.

Zorba pointed to the Cloud Police. "Take him away. Take him to the room where we encase victims

in carbonite. I'll deal with him as soon as I return from destroying the factory barge—and Princess Leia along with it!"

While those momentous events were taking place in the penthouse suite, something almost as momentous was going on in the basement of the Holiday Towers Hotel and Casino.

A human guard brought a meal to Ken in his cell. But Ken was no longer hungry. He was now feeling much more alert, less tired, and able to make a plan of action.

Ken decided to try the Jedi mind trick he'd tried on Trioculus. But this time he would use it on the guard instead.

He concentrated. Freeing his mind of all thoughts except the thought of getting free, he imagined the guard's mind emptying—entering a state of total confusion.

"Can't you see that I'm not the boy you are looking for!" Ken exclaimed. "I'm Tibor, the bounty hunter! The prisoner tricked me and locked me in here! Help me get out of here, before he gets away!"

It worked! Thinking Ken was Tibor, the guard apologized and hurriedly unlocked the cell.

Soon Ken was outside the Holiday Towers building, running through the streets of Cloud City.

He passed many dazzling sights of the big city, including Masque Hall, where he peeked through a window to see the never-ending masquerade party.

Next he stumbled upon the Central Cloud Car Taxi

Port. Unfortunately his pockets were empty. He had no credits to pay for a ride back to Han Solo's sky house.

The Jedi mind trick had worked once, so Ken tried it again on the taxi driver. And once again it worked. Ken actually convinced the taxi driver that he had already paid for the ride!

On the Imperial factory barge, Luke and Kate were searching for Princess Leia.

Luke used the macrobinoculars he had brought with him to peer in the windows of every building he could see. He was trying to find any possible clue that might lead him to the princess.

Then at last, while staring at a room on the top floor of the tallest factory, he spotted her. She was smashing a window and crawling out onto a ledge. Luke looked higher with the macrobinoculars, checking out the roof of the building. There was a platform with a hovertransport. Around the corner of the building from Leia, he saw a service ladder that went up the side of the building—a ladder that could help them get up to her!

A short time later, when Luke met up with Leia on the ledge, she was so startled she almost fell, but then regained her balance.

"Leia! At last Kate and I found you!" Luke said. "There's a ladder to the roof around the corner. Quick—follow me!"

Leia, Luke, and Kate carefully climbed the ladder up to the flat, black roof. They scurried across it and soon reached the platform with the parked hovertransport.

Luke used the macrobinoculars again, this time to scan the brown sky above the tall smokestacks, looking to see if there were any Imperial vehicles flying nearby.

But instead of an Imperial vehicle he saw the *Millennium Falcon!*

Inside the *Millennium Falcon* Han Solo and Chewbacca were weaving in and out among the smokestacks, desperately searching for Luke, Leia, and Kate.

Laser cannons from the barge fired at the *Falcon* as Han descended low enough to spot the wrecked cloud car convertible. Then suddenly he heard a communication signal and a familiar-sounding voice!

"Millennium Falcon! Do you copy? Over."

It was Luke!

"I copy," Han said. "Where are you, Luke? Over."

"Check starboard, three-five. I'm piloting the Imperial hovertransport. This thing's a puddle jumper without even enough vertical thrust to get us home."

"I'll get below you and open the hatch," Han said. "Do you think Kate can make the jump into the *Falcon*? Over."

"Of course she can," Luke replied. "We're all ready to ditch this thing and fly back in style!"

In seconds the *Millennium Falcon* was flying directly below the hovertransport, a short leap away. Leia and Kate jumped out of the hovertransport first, falling safely into the *Falcon*. Then Luke set the hovertransport on automatic pilot and made the leap too.

Ground fire continued to target them. It missed the *Millennium Falcon,* but blew the hovertransport to pieces.

Luke looked around the cockpit of the *Falcon.* "Where's Ken?" he asked. "You didn't leave him home alone, did you?"

"Don't blame me," Han said, "but Ken got behind the wheel of my Custom Model-Q Foley and zoomed off for Cloud City."

"Han, he's just a kid!" Luke protested. "He's not even thirteen years old!"

"Tell that to him," Han said. "He seems to think he's old enough to drive in the Cloud Car Racing Finals. But don't worry, I sent Threepio, Artoo, and Chip to bring him back."

When Luke, Leia, and Kate were safely seated inside the *Millennium Falcon,* a fleet of very strange

looking spaceships appeared, each one a unique model from a different planet. There were dozens of them, and most of them were out-of-date models.

It was a fleet of bounty hunter spaceships. A rag-tag fleet, the spaceships descended through the clouds until they were just above the factory barge.

Leading the pack was the ancient Huttian space-ship, the *Zorba Express.*

The *Millennium Falcon* soared away from the fac-tory barge and over the Rethin Sea, just in time to avoid being spotted by the incoming fleet. From inside the *Falcon*, Han, Chewbacca, Luke, Leia, and Kate could see the fleet of spaceships attacking the factory barge.

The spaceships attacked relentlessly, dropping ion explosives, nova bombs, and doonium acid mines.

The entire factory barge began to quiver and tremble under the shock of the tremendous blasts.

At last Zorba the Hutt scored a direct hit on the central generator building—the domed power center for the Imperial barge.

In their last look back, Han, Chewbacca, Luke, Leia, and Kate saw the factory barge splitting in two and shattering.

A huge fireball rose into the plumes of brown smoke. Han Solo could practically feel the heat of the explosion behind him as the *Millennium Falcon* flew farther and farther away.

The factory buildings, smokestacks and all, plunged down into the sea of liquid rethin, then van-ished as if they had never existed at all.

"A narrow escape, Chewie," Han said with a grin. "If I'd stopped for even half a minute to lubricate our subatomic accelerator, our friends here would still be down there, boiling in bubbling rethin."

Han wasn't the only one who was pleased with his timing. Zorba the Hutt was just as pleased, because he had information that Princess Leia was a prisoner in the tallest building on the barge, trapped in Trioculus's chambers.

And so he was convinced that Princess Leia had gone down with the factory barge, and that her mortal remains were now sinking deep into the liquid metal core of Bespin.

The death of Jabba the Hutt had been avenged!

"A-HAW-HAW-HAW!! . . ." Zorba roared.

* * *

Zorba the Hutt returned directly to Cloud City, to the very room where Darth Vader once encased Han Solo in carbonite. There Trioculus was strapped to a hydraulic platform from which he could not escape.

"Your so-called Queen of the Empire is dead, Trioculus," Zorba announced. "Princess Leia's body is now sinking into the core of the planet, along with all your factories. So the next time a Hutt offers you a fair deal—a chance to trade one life for another—think twice before you refuse it." Zorba stroked his beard and wagged his thick tongue. "But I almost forgot. There won't *be* a next time for you. A-HAW-HAW-HAW . . ."

"You've sealed your doom, Zorba!" Trioculus shouted in defiance. "An armada of Imperial starships will come to destroy you—and Cloud City!"

Zorba thumped his massive tail on the floor in anger. "When the rumor gets out that you've been encased in carbonite and hidden somewhere in Cloud City, no Imperial will dare try to blow up this city. Besides, Cloud City was armed by the Rebel Alliance before I took it over from Lando Calrissian. We'll gladly defend ourselves against any stormtrooper invasion!"

"We can still make a deal, Zorba," Trioculus said. "I could share my power with you! You could become a grand admiral in the Empire!"

"Never," Zorba replied with a scowl. "I'd rather join the Rebel Alliance than raise the tip of my tail to help you! And now if you'll excuse me, I'm going to encase you in carbonite. Your body will be frozen and trapped, and your mind will be in constant torment!" Zorba licked his cheeks with his thick tongue. "Get ready . . . get set . . ."

"No, Zorba! Stop!"

"Go!!!" Zorba threw the switch, and the hydraulic platform was dropped into the pit.

"Ahhhhhhrrrrggghhh!" Trioculus screamed, the sound growing louder and louder.

In the pit there was bubbling liquid, gaseous fumes, and huge billows of smoke.

PZZZZZZT! SIZZZZZZZ!

The deed was finished.

Just as it had once been done to Han Solo, Trioculus's body was now trapped inside a block of carbonite.

Huge metal tongs then lifted the block out of the pit. Trioculus resembled a living sculpture; all three of his eyes now stared out in horror into the blackness in front of his face.

Soon Zorba broadcast his news from Cloud City, announcing the death of the Rebel Alliance Princess who murdered Jabba the Hutt! He warned all citizens to be alert for a possible Imperial attack, because Emperor Trioculus—now encased in a block of carbonite—was about to become a permanent, heavily guarded exhibit in the Cloud City Museum.

Inside the *Millennium Falcon,* they too heard Zorba's news broadcast.

"Trioculus has been carbonized—that's the best thing that's happened since I finished building my

sky house!" Han exclaimed. "But we've got to get you off the planet, Princess. If Zorba the Hutt finds out that you're still alive, sparks are going to fly. And I don't want you to be around when the trouble starts."

Making a quick stop at Han's sky house, they picked up Ken, along with Chip, Threepio, and Artoo-Detoo. The three droids had spotted Ken returning to Han's house in the cloud taxi. As Han packed up a few things, Ken frantically told everyone about his misadventures in Cloud City.

But they didn't hang around very long. For all Han knew, bounty hunters were spying on his sky house with macrobinoculars just to make sure that Leia was really dead.

As soon as they were all aboard the *Millennium Falcon*, Han set their course, punching codes into the navigation unit without giving anyone any clues about where he was taking them.

"You haven't even had a chance to enjoy your house yet, Han," Leia said. "I'm sorry you have to leave like this."

"Your safety comes first, Princess. For the time being, I'm leaving behind the life-style of a home-owner. I'm officially a traveling man again."

"Where should we go?" Luke asked the princess. "To the Rebel Alliance Senate on Yavin Four?"

"Too many Imperials between here and Yavin Four," Leia countered.

"If they board us for an inspection and find you," Han said, "Zorba the Hutt will be one of the first to hear the news."

"*Dweeeeboo Ptwaaa!*" Artoo tooted.

"Artoo suggests that perhaps we should head for your home planet, Han," Threepio translated. "The Corellian life-style has always been agreeable to droids."

"I've got another place in mind," Han replied.

"Where exactly?" Leia asked.

"Don't you like surprises?" Han asked.

"Is it a planet?" Ken added.

"Or is it a moon?" Luke asked. "Or an asteroid?"

"Or a space station?" Ken suggested.

"Let's just say it's a romantic place," Han said with a wink.

"Romantic, Han?" Princess Leia asked, smiling.

"Yes, Princess. Any objections?"

"None that I can think of," she replied. "As long as I have my brother along to chaperon," she teased. "Okay with you, Luke?"

"Affirmative," Luke replied. "Power up and engage sublightspeed thrusters!"

And they took off.

Han's sky house quickly became a speck of dust far behind them. Moments later, so did the planet Bespin.

"Luke, take over the accelerator for a minute, okay?" Han asked.

Luke took control of the acceleration lever and Han gave Princess Leia a kiss—a very long kiss.

While he was kissing Princess Leia, a crazy

thought popped into Han Solo's mind. Maybe he should propose marriage to her. Maybe it was about time that he popped the question.

But what would he say exactly? *Senator Leia Organa, could you ever love a mischievous Corellian pilot like me enough to say "I do" at the altar?* No—too stiff and formal. How about the simple approach? *Princess, will you marry me?* Nope. Too short, not enough affection. What about *Leia, will you be my wife and the mother of my children?* No, too old-fashioned.

It was a tough problem. A very tough problem indeed.

No doubt about it, he would have to wait until some other day to figure out how to say the words in just the right way. Or the day after some other day.

Ken smiled and gave Luke Skywalker a little nudge as they watched Han and Leia embrace. Luke waited until just after Han's and Leia's lips separated before pulling on the hyperdrive thruster, boosting their velocity far above light speed.

ZWOOOOOOOSH! There was a blurry flash!

And then they were gone!

To find out more about the Rebel Alliance and how they finally meet up with Emperor Palpatine's real son, don't miss *Mission from Mount Yoda*, book four of our continuing Star Wars adventures.

Here's a preview:

Ken awoke with a churning feeling in his stomach. He was feeling upset. Luke, Leia, Han, Chewbacca, and the droids were going off to Duro without him, and Ken was being left behind to attend classes at Dagobah Tech. Ken was reluctant. Why did he have to go to school, anyway? He could learn everything he needed to know while going off on Alliance missions.

Ken washed, dressed, brushed, and combed, then he hurried outside the main DRAPAC building, running all the way to the hangar where the *Millennium Falcon* was docked on a landing pad.

Ken walked inside the hangar to see if Luke or any of the others were inside the spaceship. He popped through the hatch and airlock, but was disappointed to discover that no one else was on board. Maybe they were back in the cargo bay of the *Millennium Falcon*, near the engineering station and service access. They were probably strapping down their gear to get ready for takeoff.

Ken thought he heard the sound of boots walking near the quadrex power core. He swung around to look, accidentally knocking into a loose transport crate and toppling it against the cargo door's emergency control mechanism.

CRASH!

Suddenly the bulkhead door to the cargo bay swung shut.

FWOOOOOOP! CLIIIICK!

Uh-oh! It was locked!

"Help!" he shouted. "Can anybody hear me? I'm locked in the cargo bay and can't get out!"

Ken tried pushing on the door, then gave up, collapsing to the floor in despair. He sat there, desperately trying to think of some way to escape. Then the soft white light turned red, and the entire hold rumbled with the sudden sound of the ship's power converter and ion flux stabilizer.

The rumbling increased, and Ken was slammed against the floor of the cargo hold, pressed down by an incredibly strong pressure. Unless he was mistaken, he was now on his way to the planet Duro!

What role will Ken play in revealing the carefully guarded secret of the existence of Emperor Palpatine's real son, Triclops? And can the Imperials recapture the escaped Triclops and put an end to his hopes of taking over the Empire? Find out in *Mission from Mount Yoda*, coming soon.

Glossary

Avabush spice
A spice that acts as a truth serum, also brings on sleepiness. Often it's baked into sweets, such as candy-flavored buns.

Bantha
A mammoth creature as large as an elephant, with tremendous looped horns. Ridden by Tusken Raiders as a form of transportation.

Bespin
The giant, gaseous planet where Cloud City is located. Bespin is located in the Bespin System. It has a core of liquid rethin metal, but its prosperity comes from the resources of its Tibanna gas mines. The Empire maintains a barge on Bespin that floats just above the Rethin Sea, with many factories for making war machines.

Braze
A word that is short for "brown haze," much as the word "smog" is short for "smoke and fog."

Carbonite
A substance made from Tibanna gas, plentiful on the planet Bespin, where it is mined and sold in liquid form

as a fuel in Cloud City. When carbonite is turned into a solid, it can be used for keeping humans or other organisms alive in a state of suspended animation, encasing them completely.

CB-99
A dusty, slightly bent, old barrel-shaped droid hidden in a secret room in the palace of Jabba the Hutt. He has a hologram file containing Jabba the Hutt's will.

Chip (short for Microchip)
Ken's personal droid, who lived with him in the Lost City of the Jedi and has now gone out into the world with him.

Cloud Police
The force that keeps the peace by enforcing the laws of Cloud City. Their leader is Chief Muskov, who does the bidding of the governor of Cloud City. The Cloud Police have a tradition of trying to remain neutral between the Alliance and the Empire.

Jabba the Hutt
A sluglike alien gangster and smuggler who owned a palace on Tatooine and consorted with alien bounty hunters. He was strangled to death by Princess Leia, choked by the chain that held her prisoner in his sail barge at the Great Pit of Carkoon.

Jawa
A meter-high creature who travels the deserts of Tatooine collecting and selling scrap. It has glowing orange eyes that peer out from under its hooded robe.

Jenet
An ugly, quarrelsome alien species. Scavengers, they have pale pink skin, red eyes, and sparse white fuzz that covers their thin bodies. They are sometimes known to hang out in the Mos Eisley Cantina.

Kate (short for KT-18)
A female, pearl-colored housekeeping droid that Luke buys from jawas on Tatooine as a housewarming gift for Han Solo.

Ken
A twelve-year-old Jedi Prince, who was raised by droids in the Lost City of the Jedi. He was brought to the underground city as a small child by a Jedi Knight in a brown robe. He knows nothing of his origins, but he does know many Imperial secrets, which he learned from studying the files of the master Jedi computer in the Jedi Library where he went to school. Long an admirer of Luke Skywalker, he has departed the Lost City and joined the Alliance.

Kip
The planet where Zorba the Hutt was kept prisoner for illegally mining gemstones.

Mos Eisley
A spaceport on Tatooine, made up of low concrete structures. The cantina at the spaceport is a dangerous place, a hangout for many outlaws and fugitives.

Ranats
Cunning and small, these powerful pests are ratlike aliens, with rodent tails and sharp teeth. They have now settled into Jabba's palace on Tatooine.

Repulsorlifts
Repulsorlifts keep Han's sky house, Trioculus's factory barge, and even Cloud City floating in the air.

Rethin Sea
The liquid metal core of the planet Bespin.

Sabacc
A popular casino card game in Cloud City.

Sandcrawler
A large transport used by the jawas.

Sky house
A new concept in dwellings, invented by Han Solo and Chewbacca, it is a house that uses repulsorlifts to float in the sky. Han owns the only sky house on Bespin. It floats on a cloud on the outskirts of Cloud City.

Tatooine
A desert planet with twin suns, Tatooine is Luke Skywalker's home planet.

Tibor
A bounty hunter who hangs out at Mos Eisley on Tatooine. Tibor is a Barabel alien—a vicious, bipedal reptiloid—

who has horny green scales. He is hired by Zorba the Hutt
to assist and serve Zorba in any way the Hutt desires.

Trioculus
Three-eyed mutant who was the Supreme slavelord of
Kessel. He is now Emperor. Trioculus is a liar and impostor who claims to be the son of Emperor Palpatine. In his
rise to power he was supported by the grand moffs, who
helped him find the glove of Darth Vader, an everlasting
symbol of evil.

Tusken Raiders
Also called sand people they live a nomadic life in some
of Tatooine's most desolate deserts. Often riding on
Banthas for transportation, they are vicious desert bandits
who fear little and make frequent raids on local settlers.

Twi'lek alien
A humanoid alien with a head tentacle, he is one of the
bounty hunters who hangs out in the Mos Eisley Cantina.

Zorba Express
Zorba the Hutt's ancient bell-shaped spaceship.

Zorba the Hutt
The father of Jabba the Hutt. He was unaware of his son's
death because he had been a prisoner on the planet Kip.
Zorba looks similar to Jabba, but he has long white braided
hair and a white beard. Jabba's will leaves all of his possessions to Zorba, including Jabba's palace, and the Holiday Towers Hotel and Casino at Cloud City on Bespin.

About the Authors

PAUL DAVIDS and **HOLLACE DAVIDS** met by chance in Harvard Square in 1971, just after Paul saw George Lucas's first movie, *THX 1138*. It was love at first sight. Paul had graduated from Princeton and Hollace from Goucher and from the master's program in counseling at Boston University. But they discovered that they had grown up just a few miles apart in Bethesda and Silver Spring, Maryland. They married several months after they first met.

Paul, who began making 8mm science fiction movies when he was ten, studied writing and directing at the American Film Institute in L.A., and a few years later became a member of the Writers Guild (WGA), writing for Cornel Wilde and (with Hollace) George Pal, a pioneer of movie science fiction. After teaching children with learning disabilities, Hollace became the FILMEX Society Coordinator for the L.A. International Film Exposition.

In 1977, the year *Star Wars* premiered, their daughter Jordan was born. In 1980, the year *The Empire Strikes Back* opened, their son Scott was born, and Hollace began coordinating all the major film premieres and parties for Columbia Pictures. And when *Return of the Jedi* opened in 1983, Paul's accomplishments included writing *She Dances Alone*, a movie starring Bud Cort and Max von Sydow, and producing for the TV show *Lie Detector*. He then worked as production coordinator for about one hundred episodes of *The Transformers*, some of which he wrote. Currently Paul is an executive producer of a movie for HBO based on the book *UFO Crash at Roswell*, and Hollace is vice president of publicity and special events for TriStar Pictures.

Paul and Hollace published their first book in 1986, *The Fires of Pele*, a fantasy about Mark Twain in Hawaii. Now they are hard at work on even more Star Wars books for young readers.

About the Illustrators

KARL KESEL was born in 1959 and raised in the small town of Victor, New York. He started reading comic books at the age of ten, while traveling cross-country with his family, and decided soon after he wanted to become a cartoonist. By the age of twenty-five, he landed a full-time job as an illustrator for DC Comics, working on such titles as *Superman*, *World's Finest*, *Newsboy Legion*, and *Hawk and Dove*, which he also cowrote. He was also one of the artists on *The Terminator* and *Indiana Jones* miniseries for Dark Horse Comics. Mr. Kesel lives and works with his wife, Barbara, in Milwaukie, Oregon.

DREW STRUZAN is a teacher, lecturer, and one of the most influential forces working in commercial art today. His strong visual sense and recognizable style have produced lasting pieces of art for advertising, the recording industry, and motion pictures. His paintings include the album covers for *Alice Cooper's Greatest Hits* and *Welcome to My Nightmare,* which was recently voted one of the one hundred classic album covers of all time by *Rolling Stone* magazine. He has also created the movie posters for Star Wars, *E.T. The Extra-Terrestrial,* the Back to the Future series, the Indiana Jones series, *An American Tale,* and *Hook.* Mr. Struzan lives and works in the California valley with his wife Cheryle. Their son, Christian, is continuing in the family tradition, working as an art director and illustrator.